For Glad with love from Harry

All rights reserved. For information about permission
to reproduce selections from this book, write to
Permissions, Houghton Mifflin Company, 2 Park Street,
Boston, Massachusetts 02108

Printed in Hong Kong by Imago Services (H.K.) Ltd.

10 9 8 7 6 5 4 3 2 1

Cataloging-in-Publication Data is available from the Library of Congress.

Splodger

Paul Dowling

Houghton Mifflin Company

Boston 1991

"It's bedtime, Kate," said Dad.

Kate slid off her chair and hid under the table.

"I said bed, Kate," said Dad.

"Grrr!" said Kate. "Dad told me to go to bed, but I'm not Kate anymore..."

"I'm SPLODGER!

And Splodger doesn't go to bed.
Splodger stays up.

Splodger does everything children
aren't allowed to do!"

Splodger stuck out her tongue.

"Splodger can stick out her tongue," said Splodger.

"And make rude noises. THURRRRRRPPP!"

Splodger ran into the garden...

SPLUDGE!

"Splodger jumps in puddles with her slippers on," said Splodger, "and she never wipes her feet!"

"Who brought all this mud in?" shouted Mom.

"Splodger did!" shouted Splodger.

"Splodger talks with her mouth full and she never eats her crusts!" spluttered Splodger with a mouth full of Dad's sandwich.

"Hey, that's my sandwich!" yelled Dad.

Splodger ran into the living room and stood right in front of the television.

"K-a-a-t-e! Get out of the way," shouted Kate's big brother.

"I'm not Kate, I'm Splodger," shouted Splodger.

Splodger collected up all her toys.

"Splodger never shares her toys
with anybody!" said Splodger.

So she carried everything
upstairs...

And dropped them all over the
bedroom floor.

"Splodger never puts anything
away," said Splodger.

"Splodger never ever hangs
up her clothes!"

"And Splodger never, ever, ever makes her bed!"

She pulled her bedcovers off and landed on the floor with all her toys and clothes and boots and everything.

WHAT A MESS!

"Who made all this mess?"
asked Mom.

"Splodger did," said a voice from
under the mess.

"Well, Splodger's got some
cleaning up to do," said Mom.

"But, Mom . . ." said the voice.

"I'm not Splodger anymore—I'm Kate!"